THE
WHEREWOOD

GABRIELLE PRENDERGAST

Orca currents

ORCA BOOK PUBLISHERS

Published in Canada and the United States in 2021 by Orca Book Publishers.
orcabook.com

Library and Archives Canada Cataloguing in Publication
Title: The wherewood / Gabrielle Prendergast.
Names: Prendergast, Gabrielle, author.
Series: Orca currents.
Description: Series statement: Orca Currents
Identifiers: Canadiana (print) 20210095296 | Canadiana (ebook) 202100953OX |
ISBN 9781459828049 (softcover) | ISBN 9781459828056 (PDF) |
ISBN 9781459828063 (EPUB)
Classification: LCC PS8631.R448 W44 2021 | DDC jc813/.6—dc23

Library of Congress Control Number: 2020951480

Summary: In this high-interest accessible novel for middle-grade readers,
14-year-old Blue Jasper goes on another Faerie Woods adventure,
to the Wherewood, the forest of lost things.

Orca Book Publishers is committed to reducing the consumption of
nonrenewable resources in the making of our books. We make
every effort to use materials that support a sustainable future.

Orca Book Publishers gratefully acknowledges the support for its publishing
programs provided by the following agencies: the Government of Canada,
the Canada Council for the Arts and the Province of British Columbia
through the BC Arts Council and the Book Publishing Tax Credit.

Edited by Tanya Trafford
Design by Ella Collier
Cover photograph by Getty Images/serts and Unsplash.com/Nick Baker
Author photo by Erika Forest

Printed and bound in Canada.

24 23 22 21 • 1 2 3 4

Chapter One

I made a deal with a Faerie. A Nixie, to be exact. That's a water Faerie. I should have known better. My mother told me not to make deals with Faeries. She said they never turn out well. She was right.

I accidentally made a deal with a Nixie called Salix. We're sort of friends. Salix says friendship with Faeries is always a bit tricky. Now, because of that deal, I'm on my way back into Faerieland. Faeries call their lands "woods." Salix and I are heading to a place called the Crosswood. It's where you cross over from the human world to the Faerie world. And it's magic, in case you were wondering.

A month ago I had no idea magic or Faeries even existed. I thought I was just a normal kid with a pretty normal family.

Ha! Wrong!

It turns out my younger brother and sister are adopted, kind of. Indigo and Violet are their names. They're nearly ten, and they're twins. My mother, Jules Jasper, has raised them since they were babies. I was about four years old when they came into our lives. Now I'm fourteen. Indigo and Violet's real mother is Olea. She used to be a Faerie queen.

I know. Weird, right?

A month ago, Olea's rival, a Faerie king called Oren, kidnapped Indigo and Violet. Then, because of magic, I had to go rescue them.

I had no choice. It was the kind of magic that kills people. I went into the Crosswood to look for them. That's where I met Salix. I asked him for help finding the twins. He tricked me into making a deal. He said he would help me if I gave him something. I thought he meant a juice box! But he didn't. He was saving that "something" for later.

Turns out that "something" is my going on a quest with him. It's going to be dangerous. And I will be missing school. And my mom is going to be mad at me.

But that's what happens when you make deals with Faeries. You have to stick to them—or else.

And by the way, crossing from the human world to the Faerie world is very uncomfortable. It feels a bit like how it must feel to be swallowed. You get sucked down into the earth. You slither around underground like a worm. If you're not careful you get mud in your mouth. Then you pop out the other side. For a few seconds everything is upside down. You feel like you're walking on the ceiling. But after a moment or two something clicks in your brain. Then everything is right side up again.

That's what just happened to me.

Salix and my other Faerie friend, Finola, brush dirt off me as I stand up. Salix looks a bit like a frog. His hair and eyes are bright green like grass. His skin is slightly green too. Maybe all Nixies look like him. I don't know. He's the only one I've met so far.

Finola looks a bit like a swan. Actually she used to *be* a swan. A witch cursed her. I helped undo the curse. Long story. Her skin is very pale, but her hair and eyes are shiny black. She also has a crown made of white feathers, a leftover from the witch's enchantment.

Salix carries a small lantern. Finola has a sword. All I have are my backpack and some cupcakes. Doesn't seem like quite enough for a quest.

Our quest is to find the way into Salix's home wood. That's why I'm here in the Crosswood again.

I should be mad at Salix for dragging me along. But I'm not. A Faerie quest is a lot better than chores and school. To be honest, I'm not enjoying high school very much. I keep getting into trouble. I'm not good at making friends. And there's a lot of homework. It's stressful. I've even been having trouble sleeping.

"What is this wood of yours called anyway?" I ask as we set off. "If I'm going to help you look for it, I should at least know what it's called."

"Merwood," Salix says.

"Merwood," I repeat. "And you said it's a few days' walk from here?"

"At least," Finola says. Salix nudges her. I can tell they aren't telling me everything. That's just the way Faeries are. I'm getting used to it.

"We should go over the rules again," Salix says. "Since you'll be here in the Faerie Woods for a while."

"Probably smart," I say.

So as we walk, Salix and Finola remind me of a few things about Faeries. How they can't lie, for example. How if you know a Faerie's full name, you can command them to give you three wishes.

"That only works once though, remember?" Finola reminds me. "So you can never use it on me again."

That's how I helped her turn back into a human. You can command them to do anything with your three wishes. Even magic stuff. Only humans can do it though. That's why Faeries try never to let humans learn their full names.

"Yeah, I remember all this stuff," I say. "But is there anything *new* I should know?"

Salix scratches his green hair with one webbed hand. "As long as you're with us, you'll be safe," he says. "Although you should always watch out for wild magic."

"Oh yeah," Finola says. "You need to be *very* careful of that!"

"What's wild magic?" I ask. It sounds a bit scary.

"Sometimes when a Faerie does magic, a bit of it escapes," Finola says.

"And it can get into other things," Salix says. "And make them do magical things."

"Like...toadstools," Finola says. "Remember, Salix, what happened to King Oren's rug?"

"Hmmm," Salix says. "That was an accident."

Finola and I giggle. The Faerie Woods can be scary sometimes. But they're fun too. I'm about to ask for more information about wild magic when...

"Salix Flapfoot! What have you done?"

$$\rightarrow \star \leftarrow$$

We all stumble to a stop. Oren, the Faerie King of Farwood, has suddenly appeared. It is like he popped out of the ground.

Salix drops to one knee and bows his head.

"Your Majesty," he says.

"Stand up, idiot child," Oren says. I don't know why he calls Salix "child." Oren doesn't look like he's much older than me.

Salix stands. His green face grows pink with shame.

"Why is Blue Jasper here?" Oren asks. "Didn't I say the human should stay away from the Faerie Woods?"

"You did, but..."

Oren is angry. Not so much at me though. He's half brother to Indigo and Violet. That makes him my brother too, in a way. He's angry at Salix for bringing me here. And once Salix explains, Oren knows about our deal, a Faerie pact. It means I had no choice in the matter.

It's nice for someone else to be in trouble for a change. Now that I'm here, I realize I don't want to go home.

"He asked me to help find his wood," I say. "I'd like to help. No one should be without a home."

Oren raises his eyebrows at me. He looks amused. With Faeries that's usually not good.

"I suppose Salix hasn't told you very much about Merwood," Oren says.

"Uh-oh," Finola says.

"No, but..." Now I'm annoyed. I know it's going to be something bad. I turn to Salix and glare at him. He shrugs.

"Merwood is an Unseelie wood," Oren says.

"What does 'Unseelie' mean?" I ask.

"Seelie and Unseelie are the two types of Faerie kingdoms. The words are old. And hard to translate," Oren says. "Once they meant 'happy' and 'unhappy.' Or close to that."

"And now?" I ask.

"They don't mean anything," Salix says quickly. "At least, they don't mean what they used to. Those divisions don't matter anymore."

"So says you, Salix Flapfoot," Oren says. "Long ago, the Unseelie woods waged a wicked war on the

9

Seelie woods, Nearwood and Farwood. When they lost the war, the Unseelie woods were cursed. Merwood was cursed for one hundred years. Fenwood was cursed for one thousand years. And Witherwood..." His face hardens. It's difficult for him to speak of anything to do with Olea. "Witherwood was cursed for all time," he finishes.

"Wait," I say. "Merwood is connected to Witherwood?"

Witherwood is where Olea was sent as punishment for her crimes. She killed Oren's father, who was also the father of Indigo and Violet. Olea is a very bad Faerie. She nearly killed my mother. She nearly killed me. I'd rather not get anywhere near her. "Is this true, Salix? Is Merwood connected to Witherwood?"

He shrugs, looking guilty. "Sort of?"

"Salix!" I cry.

Oren sighs again. "One day, little Flapfoot, I will be rid of your mischief."

Salix grins, even though he's in trouble. "If I can find the way back into Merwood, you will!" he says happily.

Oren rolls his eyes. "I suppose that's true," he says. "The most likely place to start looking is the Wherewood. But that is still a long way from here." He looks around. "And it will be dark soon. Come to my court to eat and sleep. In the morning we can discuss what to do next."

Chapter Two

Oren's court is in a huge castle. I've been here before. That time, though, I was brought in as a prisoner. This time I feel much more welcome. Little Faerie servants come and take my backpack and hoodie. We pass a fountain in the center of a large courtyard. Oren and his guards stop to wash their hands and faces. Salix and Finola do the same. So I join them.

The water smells of strawberries and cream and sunshine. And it's warm. Like most teenagers, I have a few pimples. But after I wash my face in the fountain, my skin is smooth. I glance up into the polished silver trim on the fountain. Yep. No zits. I need a fountain like this at home.

Feeling fresh and clean, I follow Oren through a long passageway. Along the walls there are paintings of various magical creatures. Unicorns. Dragons. And Faeries. I wonder if they are Oren's ancestors. They'd be Indigo and Violet's ancestors too. Weird.

The passage opens into Oren's Great Hall. This is where his throne is. This is where he holds court. Oren's hall is inside his castle. But it looks like it's outside. The walls are made of live trees. Their branches wind together and form the ceiling.

Last time I was in Oren's Great Hall, Faeries and other creatures were milling around. Some of them were sleeping. Some of them were having picnics on the floor.

This time they are all seated at a long table. The table is loaded with food! So much amazing food! All the creatures are eating and talking and laughing. No one seems to notice us. Oren pauses just inside the hall.

"Don't anyone get up for me," he says. "I'm only your king."

All the guests ignore him. They keep eating and enjoying themselves. You'd think they'd have more respect for him. Maybe things aren't like that in the Faerie Woods.

Oren sighs.

"Come on," he says. "Let's find you somewhere to sit."

"Where are Indigo and Violet?" I ask. Indigo and Violet live in the Faerie realm during the week. They live at my house with Mom and me on the weekends.

"Violet is in Nearwood tonight," Oren says.

That makes sense. Violet is the queen of Nearwood now. Maybe Indigo is with her.

"Indigo put a growth charm on my favorite rosebush," Oren continues. "It burst into flames. So tonight he's having dinner in his room."

I try not to laugh. Indigo is just as bratty here as he is at home.

Oren takes his place at the head of the table. He shoves two Faeries and a Troll down a few spaces so Finola, Salix and I can sit.

Salix and Finola start eating straight away. They put piles of berries and cakes onto their plates. I've been warned not to eat Faerie food. It makes humans lose their minds. That's the last thing I need.

Oren grins at me as he fills his own plate.

"The meatballs are safe for you," he says, pointing to a bowl. "I get them from IKEA."

I spoon a few onto my plate. Sure enough, they taste just like IKEA meatballs. Oren also has a servant bring me a bottle of ginger ale, some yogurt tubes and a tin of English shortbread. As I eat, the servants keep bringing me more things. Most of them are still in the packets. Ordinary grocery-store things like cereal, cookies and chips. Stuff Mom never lets me eat at home.

At Mom's, everything is homemade and organic. It is good, and I am never hungry or anything. But this is incredible. I eat as much as I can, and before long I'm stuffed.

⇒ ★ ⇐

Gradually the table clears as Finola, Salix and all the other Faeries drift away. Many of them curl up on the floor or under a tree to go to sleep. But I'm wide awake. I've never eaten so much sugar in my life. Oren leans back in his chair, rubbing his stomach.

"I'm afraid the magic of the Woods may require you to complete Salix's quest with him," he says.

"I figured that," I reply.

"I wish Salix had waited," Oren says. "At least until things were more…settled."

"You mean Olea," I say.

"She is gone, of course," Oren says. "Trapped in Witherwood. But she has supporters. You will have to be careful."

"If only I had magical powers," I say before I can stop myself.

Oren gazes at me. "Magic can be a curse as well as a blessing," he says thoughtfully.

I scoff. "If it was a curse, wouldn't Faeries just give it up? Couldn't they just...hex their magic away?"

Oren laughs so heartily that several Faeries sleeping nearby stir. They tell him to be quiet. He lowers his voice.

"That is not a magical skill we have," he says. "There is only one way we can do things we lack the magical skills for. That is if a human commands us."

"So if I had commanded Olea to lose her magical powers, she would have?" I ask.

Oren smiles. "Now you know why Faeries don't like humans to know their full names. But that would have been very dangerous. Bad things happen when magic escapes its bounds."

"Are you talking about wild magic?" I ask. "Finola and Salix told me about that."

"Exactly," Oren says. "Wild magic finds the nearest non-magical thing and rushes into it. It would have rushed into you. That could have killed you."

"Could have?" I ask. "What if it didn't? Would I be magic now?"

Oren shakes his head. "You humans are all the same," he says. "Always wanting what someone else has."

I feel myself blushing. But why should I be embarrassed? Who wouldn't want magical powers?

Oren puts his hand on my shoulder. "Magic is like blood," he says. "A human can lose blood. Or even donate it. Your body makes more. It takes time. And it might weaken you. But if you lose all your blood, you die. For Faeries, magic is like this. If we use up a large amount of magic, we eventually can make more. If we lose all our magic, we don't die. But the part of us that is Faerie dies. We become like humans."

"So how does Faerie magic work in a human?" I ask, more interested in that than Oren's Faerie lesson. "Are you saying it *wouldn't* make me magic?"

"It would, but only very briefly," Oren says. "Any magic you used would be gone. Your human body could never make more. Any big spells, like healing wounds, for example, would use it all up."

I think about this. It still seems to me that it might be worth it. Oren frowns at me. He knows what I'm thinking.

"Humans," he says, shaking his head again. "Always willing to risk so much for so little." Before I can protest, Oren calls a servant over. "Find Blue Jasper somewhere comfortable to sleep. And see that he does sleep. He'll need to be rested for his journey."

I want to prove to Oren that I'm *not* just an annoying, predictable human. So I go with the little servant without complaining. A few minutes later I'm in the most comfortable bed I've ever known. I lie there watching the magical stars on the ceiling. They twinkle through the tree branches. My eyes get heavy. I wonder if this is magic or if I'm just tired.

In under a minute I'm fast asleep.

Chapter Three

The breakfast feast is nearly as big as the dinner feast. Finola and Salix stuff themselves on little blue eggs and bright purple porridge. Oren gives me a box of toaster waffles. Then he uses magic to make a tiny fire in a teacup. I toast my waffles over it with a fork.

Two servants bring me a giant silver tray. There is a small can of orange soda on it. Everyone watches me drink it. They cheer when the bubbles make me burp.

Mealtimes are weird in Faerieland.

After breakfast Oren sees us off at the castle gate. He has decided Indigo will go with us.

"I've looked at the Faerie laws," Oren says. "Blue will go with Salix to the entrance of the Wherewood. I believe the Woods will see that as your pact fulfilled." He frowns at Indigo. "After that, Indigo will escort Blue back to the human realm. While he's there he will stop in at—" He turns to one of his guards. "What is the name of that place?"

"Garden Depot," the guard whispers.

Oren nods. "Ah, yes. Garden Depot. Indigo will stop there and buy me a new rosebush."

Salix laughs. He quickly covers it by pretending to cough.

While Finola and Salix check their supplies, Oren takes me aside. When no one is looking, he presses something into my hand. I look down. A sword and scabbard shimmer into view. The ghost sword!

The ghost sword is visible only to the person using it. Back when Finola was a swan, and I commanded her by using her full name, she had to grant me three wishes. After I'd turned her back into her original form, I commanded her some new clothes. Finally I asked her for an invisible sword. That was the ghost sword. I used it to help defeat Olea. But I didn't feel comfortable carrying it. I really don't like any kind of violence.

I gave the ghost sword to Oren. Now he's giving it back to me.

"A loan," he says. "I hope you won't need to use it. You'll only be in Farwood and the Crosswood, but still. I want you to be safe. Indigo can bring the sword back to me."

"Thank you," I whisper.

We set off, slipping by magic back into the Crosswood. Then we continue on foot. Hours pass. Indigo chatters away about nothing. I notice that Salix and Finola sometimes walk holding hands.

"Are you together?" I ask finally. "Like a couple?"

"Yes," says Salix.

"No," says Finola.

"Forget I asked," I say.

Indigo snorts with laughter. It's nice to see that romance is just as dumb in Faerieland as it is in the human world.

It's nearly dusk when Salix spots something through the dense trees.

"There it is!" he cries.

Indigo starts running.

"Stop!" I yell, chasing after him.

He's still ahead of me when we reach a clearing in the trees. On the other side of the clearing is an old VW van. It's tangled in a dense hedge. It looks a lot like the one Mom used to have. Hers was pale blue. This one is bright yellow.

Indigo yanks open the passenger door. He climbs in.

"No, Indigo!" Finola yells.

The door slams closed behind him.

The three of us arrive at the clearing together. Salix and Finola trip on a tree root. They go flying. I keep running. When I reach the van, I tug the door open.

"Indigo!" I yell. It's dark inside the van. Indigo is probably hiding in a corner somewhere. I climb in. The door slams behind me. The door on the other side of the van opens. Indigo is standing outside. The forest around him looks different. I don't pay much attention to it though. I jump out and grab his arm.

"Don't run off like that," I say angrily. Last time Indigo ran off (with Violet), Oren kidnapped him.

And Olea nearly killed Mom and me. I'd rather not repeat that.

I turn to drag him back through the van.

But the van is gone.

"What the...?" I say.

I spin around, dragging Indigo with me.

"Cool!" Indigo says. "We're in the Wherewood."

"Great," I say, rolling my eyes. "But *where* is the van?"

"The van is the way into the Wherewood," Indigo says happily. "But once you're in the Wherewood, you can't get out. Not until you find what you're looking for."

"I'm looking for the van!" I shout.

"I don't think it works that way," Indigo says.

I gaze around at the trees. They look weird. Not right. I don't want to go too far. I look at the tree closest to us. It seems to have keys instead of leaves. When I look down at my feet, I see the ground is made of something soft. I crouch to get a closer look. It's clothes! Jackets and sweaters and mittens!

"What exactly is the Wherewood?" I ask. I realize I should have asked this before.

"It's the place where lost things go," Indigo says lightly. "There's loads of lost stuff from the human world here. Ooh, look! I found a Frisbee!" He flings it away. It sails through the trees and disappears.

I spin when I hear a noise behind us. My hand grabs the hilt of the ghost sword. There's a ripple of light. I step in front of Indigo. But it's only Finola and Salix. They pop out of thin air like bubbles and tumble onto the ground.

"Ah," Salix says. "This is awkward."

"Has Indigo explained about the Wherewood?" Finola asks.

"He has," I say. "I sure wish I'd had the information earlier."

They stand, brushing lost bus tickets off their knees.

"Oren is going to be so angry," Finola says.

"It's my fault," Indigo says. He shrugs. "But Oren is always angry at me, so it doesn't matter."

I close my eyes for a second. I know how Oren feels. "How does this work exactly?" I ask. "How does the Wherewood know what you're looking for? And what happens when you find it?"

Salix rubs his chin with one webbed finger. "I'm not sure how the Wherewood knows. Some kind of magic, I guess. But I've heard that once you find the thing you're looking for, it just kind of…lets you go."

"You feel it," Finola says. "I came here when I was little. I was looking for a bracelet I lost. Once I found it I felt…light. And then I was able to use magic to slip back into the Crosswood."

I think about that for a moment. "So the Wherewood won't let me go until I find…what?

28

The entrance to Merwood? Or will I have to go into Merwood itself before I can get out?"

Salix and Finola exchange another look. I hate it when they do that.

"What is it this time?" I ask.

Salix's green skin goes pink again. "Merwood is a different kind of wood," he says.

"Different how?" I ask. I'm sure I'm not going to like the answer.

Salix hesitates. "It's…uh…kind of underwater."

Chapter Four

"*Underwater?*" I say. "How can a wood be underwater?"

Indigo makes a face. "Have you looked around? How can a tree have keys instead of leaves? How am I standing in a suitcase full of Grand Canyon T-shirts? This is Faerieland."

Indigo digs through the suitcase of T-shirts as Salix tries to explain.

"The Faeries of Merwood are Nixies—water Faeries. The forest we live in is flooded. The roots and the lower parts of the trees are all underwater."

"So...you're like fish?" I ask.

"More like frogs," Salix says. "We absorb the oxygen in water through our skin. We can stay underwater for a long time. But not forever. Only a few hours."

"Cool," I can't help saying. This is another Faerie skill I'd like to have. I'm an okay swimmer. But if I could stay underwater for a long time, I could hunt for sunken treasure and stuff.

Finola huffs impatiently. "The point is, the entrance to Merwood might be underwater. If it's deep underwater, Blue could drown."

Salix's face falls. "Yes, I just realized that."

"Maybe the Wherewood will release me before that," I say. "Maybe I won't have to go all the way into Merwood."

Finola looks worried. "Maybe. But if it doesn't, you could be stuck in the Wherewood forever. Unless you get into Merwood. Where you could drown."

Great choices. "What about you?" I ask. "Won't you drown too? Or Indigo?" I'm starting to get really angry with Salix. He shouldn't have brought us here.

"I can use magic to breathe underwater," Indigo says. He's now wearing a Grand Canyon T-shirt that's at least five sizes too big for him. It goes down to his knees. "For a while anyway. Oren showed me and Violet how. He didn't want us to drown in the castle pond."

"Yes," says Finola. "I know how to do this too. But that magic won't work on you, Blue. You're human."

I groan. I'm frustrated. As usual. I turn to Salix. "What if I commanded you?" I ask. "Using your full name?"

Salix's eyes widen. "But you don't know my full

name," he says. "I—my mother told me never to tell a human my full name."

"I know Indigo's full name though," I say. "What if I commanded him?"

Indigo tilts his head to the side. "That might work," he says. "You could command me to turn you into a frog. But how would I turn you back?"

"I'd command you again, of course," I say.

The three of them fall silent. Their faces grow very serious.

"But Blue," Finola says. "How would you command Indigo if you were a frog? Frogs can't talk."

I get a sudden chill. Faerie magic is so dangerous. What if I'd commanded Indigo to turn me into a frog without thinking of this? Would I have been stuck as a frog forever?

"Okay," I say, concentrating. "What if I just commanded Indigo to make me so I could breathe underwater? I wouldn't have to be a frog."

The three Faeries look at each other.

"I wouldn't do that," Finola says. "Unless you were very specific, the magic could go very wrong. It might choose to make you a fish or an eel."

"Or a sea slug," Indigo suggests. "Or a lobster!"

"Okay. I get it," I say. "Bad idea. But isn't there some way to do it safely? A way to make it so I can breathe underwater?"

"Well," Finola says, "we could find a witch. Witches have much better control over their magic. And they can make potions and spells that wear off."

A cool breeze suddenly blows around us. It makes the keys tinkle on the trees. It gives me another chill. Finola looks up at the sky. She frowns.

"Where are we going to find a witch?" I ask nervously.

Salix looks grim. He shines his little lantern into the dark trees.

"Witches love the Wherewood," he says. "They find all sorts of lost things for their spells and potions in here."

"That's right," Finola says. "If we stay here long enough, chances are, a witch will find us."

⇒ ★ ⇐

We decide to venture deeper into the Wherewood. The going is rough. The forest floor is made up of shoelaces and socks and lunch boxes. Every few minutes I almost trip or get tangled in something. Indigo wanders ahead. He keeps exclaiming whenever he finds something interesting.

"Hey! It's an iPod!" he says at one point. And then, "Look! This baseball is autographed!"

Finally, when my nerves are about to snap, Indigo yells, "I FOUND MY YO-YO!"

When I catch up to him, he's dancing around, waving a cheap plastic yo-yo in the air.

"I've been looking for this for ages!" he says.

He jumps up and down. A cool breeze ruffles his golden curls. I can't help but laugh along with him. He looks so happy.

As he settles down I hear a dog bark.

"What was that?" Salix asks. He takes Finola's hand again.

"It sounded like a dog," I say.

"A dog?" Finola says. "There are no dogs in the Faerie Woods."

I think about that for a second. "This one must be lost," I say. "That's why it's in the Wherewood. Right?"

The dog barks again. Closer this time.

"This way!" I shout, following the barking.

A few minutes later Indigo and I find the dog. It bounds up to me happily, wagging its tail. Taking a closer look, I see the dog is a girl. She's large, brown and shaggy. Though she's not wearing a collar, she has an envelope in her mouth. There's a name and address on it.

"*Mrs. Rosa Guzman*," I read. The address is in a city not far from where I live. "Poor puppy," I say, ruffling the dog's ears. "Are you lost?"

The dog barks.

"Let's call her Rosa," Indigo says.

"Good idea."

Turning, I see Finola and Salix hiding behind a tree.

"Don't be scared," I say. "She's friendly."

Finola and Salix step forward slowly. Rosa sniffs them. She wags her tail. I tuck the envelope into my pocket. Maybe I can take Rosa back to the human world with me. I could return her to her owners.

Salix pats Rosa's back.

"She's so soft," he says. "I heard dogs had spines like dragons."

"No, they—*what*?" I say.

"I heard they breathed poisonous gas," Finola says.

Indigo and I look at each other. He shrugs.

"I mean, her breath does kind of smell," he says.

I dig into the carpet of lost things on the forest floor and come up with a studded belt. Using my ghost sword, I cut it shorter and turn it into a collar for Rosa. Then I find a long skipping rope. I tie that to the collar as a leash. Now Rosa is ready to travel with us. At least she won't get lost again.

I'm not sure which direction to go. No one else seems to have any idea either. But Rosa starts to tug on her leash. So we follow her. She takes us into a darker part of the forest. We try to stick close together. Salix holds up his lantern to light our way. We end up on a narrow path through dense trees.

Suddenly a tall man appears out of nowhere. He's wearing a long, gold-trimmed blue coat. His hair is white and curled at the ends. And he is pointing a huge silver sword directly at us!

"Halt!" he yells. "Halt in the name of the Thirteen Colonies!"

We halt. Salix holds his lantern up a little higher.

"Who is this?" he asks.

"I'm not sure," I say, squinting up at the man. "But I think it might be George Washington."

Chapter Five

"That's *General* George Washington to you, young sir," the man says.

"General?" I ask. "Not president?"

"What?" he snaps.

"Never mind," I say.

The man's body shimmers a bit. I can see right through him for a second. Is he a ghost?

"Halt!" he shouts again. It's as though he's just noticed us.

I look around at the others. I expect things in the Faerie realm to be weird. But this is extra weird.

"I think I know what's going on," Finola says. "Last time I was in the Wherewood, I met two men. They were arguing about who would arrive in London first. And something about a slow train from Oxford and a fast train from York."

"British spies, no doubt," George Washington says.

Finola ignores him. "The men started talking about how far it was. And how fast the trains would go. Then they came up with an answer and *poof*. They disappeared."

I scratch my head. Something about her story sounds familiar. "Wait," I say. "That sounds like a math problem."

"I get it!" Indigo says. "It's homework. Lost homework."

"Exactly," Finola says. "Like you humans do at school. Someone loses their homework. It shows up here in the Wherewood. Kind of a ghost."

George Washington glares down at me. "Are you a patriot?" he asks.

"Oh...I'm not sure," I say.

"Can you tell me the locations of the British forts?" he asks.

I try to remember my history homework. "Uh...north?" I say. I probably got that wrong. But this isn't the real George Washington, so I don't think it matters.

"Not helpful," he says. "I intend to march south. What say you to that?"

"Yes! Good idea," I say. "Head south and...cross the Delaware River!" I can't believe I'm having a conversation with George Washington. But maybe if I give him the right answers, he'll let us pass. That seems like the kind of dumb thing that would happen in Faerieland.

"The Delaware River, you say?" He seems to think about it. "Are you trying to trick me? Is it a trap?"

Gah! I wish I had paid more attention in history class. *Was* the Delaware River a trap? I don't even know. "Maybe you should ask one of your advisers," I say. Then I struggle to remember any names from the American Revolution. "Like...Alexander Hamilton!"

George Washington shimmers again. He goes transparent.

"Halt!" he repeats for a third time, raising his sword.

Indigo snorts with laughter. I'm glad someone is having a good time.

"Any ideas?" I ask.

Finola and Salix both shrug. "Maybe we could just go another way," Salix says. "Or find another path."

We turn around. But we don't get more than a few feet. Two horsemen gallop toward us. They stop their horses. Now we're surrounded. Salix lifts his lantern up. I get a better look at them. My heart sinks.

I'm pretty sure one of them is Winston Churchill. The other one looks like Genghis Khan. Churchill waves an old-style pistol at us.

"Come on, lads!" he shouts. "We shall fight in the fields and in the streets. We shall fight in the hills. We shall never surrender!"

"What?" Salix says.

Genghis Khan shouts back at him angrily. I don't understand the language he's speaking, but clearly he disagrees. I have a feeling a small war is about to break out.

There's a noise in the trees. Three figures on squeaky bicycles come rolling through the undergrowth. I think I must be getting the hang of this ghost homework thing. I recognize all three of them. One is Louis Riel. Another is Gandhi. Leading them, a flaming torch in her hand, is Harriet Tubman!

All six of the homework ghosts charge into each other. I grab Indigo and Rosa. We duck. Salix pulls

Finola down. The ghosts crash together. There's a huge noise and a flash of light. I'm blinded for a second.

When my vision clears, the ghosts are gone.

The forest is full of singed homework sheets. One flutters down near me. I pick it up. It's an American Revolution word search. *Delaware* is circled. So is *Hamilton.* I toss it away.

"Now what?" I ask. I just hope we don't run into any chemistry homework. That could be dangerous. Rosa barks and pulls on her leash. She tugs me along. The others follow.

"Where is she taking us?" Finola asks.

"No idea!" I yell back.

Rosa jumps over tangles of cables. I nearly trip on a pair of headphones. Suddenly I see another ghost ahead of us. Or *is* it a ghost?

"Is that a witch?" Salix asks.

The ghost looks a bit like a witch. She's wearing a long black dress. But her bonnet is white. She looks like someone from an old-fashioned painting.

Rosa tugs hard on the leash. It jerks out of my hand.

"Rosa, no!"

But I can't stop her. She bounds after the witch. In seconds she catches her. Rosa jumps up. The woman screams. There's another flash of light. The woman disappears in a puff of worksheets.

I run to grab Rosa's leash. Indigo, Finola and Salix catch up to me.

"I guess that wasn't a real witch," Finola says.

"No," I say. "But what's this?"

Rosa has a piece of paper in her mouth. I carefully pull it out. It's soggy, but I can still read the writing.

"*Name the winds. Name the seasons,*" I read. "*Speak your name. Speak your reasons.*" I look up at Finola, Indigo and Salix. "What does that mean?" I ask.

"That's a spell," Finola says. She's excited. "I think it will summon a witch."

"Well done, Rosa," Indigo says. "What a smart dog."

Rosa wags her tail. I'm not sure though. Do I really want to summon a witch?

"Name your reasons," Salix says. "Does that mean you can just ask for something? That's what we need."

"Are you sure it's not a trick?" I ask. "It seems a little easy."

"That's how the Wherewood works," Finola says. "There's all kinds of weird magic here. It helps you. It actually wants you to find things."

I'm still doubtful. But I'll have to try it. I want to go home eventually. So I have to get Salix into Merwood. I don't want to drown doing it. I twist Rosa's leash around my wrist.

I look at the spell again. "It says *the winds*. That's the directions, right? North, south and that?"

Finola nods.

"Okay then." I take a breath. "North, south, east, west. Winter, spring, summer, fall. My name is Blue Jasper. I need a spell to breathe underwater."

For a second nothing happens.

Then *everything* happens.

A huge wind blows up. The homework sheets fly everywhere. Lightning crackles above us. The ground shakes. Finola and Salix clutch each other. Rosa cowers between my legs. Even Indigo seems scared. He takes my hand. I rest my other hand on the hilt of the ghost sword.

Suddenly a puff of purple smoke rises up from the ground. It smells of chocolate and chili peppers. We all cough, even Rosa. When the smoke clears, a woman is standing there.

She is tall and thin. Her shiny silver hair hangs down to her waist. Her eyes are bright green. Her purple and red dress blows around her. A black cape flutters behind her.

It's the witch!

Chapter Six

The witch looks around at all of us. She sighs.

"I'm supposed to say some creepy stuff. *Toil and trouble* and all that. Try to scare you," she says. "I can't be bothered. What do you want?"

Well. That's not what I expected. But I can work with this. I hold out my hand.

"Hi," I say. "I'm Blue Jasper."

She looks at my hand for a second. Then she reaches forward and places a single marble in my palm.

"Uh...thank you?" I try. "Did you hear my request?"

"Yes, yes," she says impatiently. "You want to breathe underwater. Who doesn't?"

I put the marble in my pocket. "Is that a spell you can do though? Safely? I don't want to turn into a frog and stay that way."

The witch laughs. I can see into her mouth. Several of her teeth are bright blue.

"Of course it's safe," she says. "Perfectly safe. But it will cost you. What do you have to trade?"

I look around at the others. We've already eaten my mom's cupcakes. I have a few bits of junk food, but I might need them later. Salix needs his lantern. Finola needs her sword. I certainly don't want to give up the ghost sword. I doubt Indigo wants to give up his yo-yo. Rosa barks happily.

The witch looks down at her.

"Is that a dog?" she asks. "From the human world?"

I don't like the hungry way the witch looks at Rosa. Is she thinking of eating her?

"She's my dog," I say quickly. "She's not for sale. Or for trade."

"Too bad," the witch says. "So many spells use eye of dog. Or tail of dog. Or liver of—"

"Not for trade!" I repeat.

Rosa whines and hides behind me.

"Oh well," says the witch. She narrows her eyes at Salix. "Are you going to this one's wood? Merwood?"

Salix crosses his arms. "Maybe. Do you know where the entrance is?"

"Not exactly," the witch says lightly. "But the Will-o'-the-Wisps like the swampy woods. I suggest you follow one. Have fun drowning." She raises one hand like she's going to do magic.

"Wait!" I shout. I need that spell. "What about hair of dog? That can be used in potions, can't it?"

"Yes." Finola nods vigorously. "Hair of dog is very...magical. Everyone knows that."

"Hair of dog?" The witch frowns down at Rosa. "I've never heard of that. What potions is it used in?"

"Lots of stuff," I say, playing along. "Cure for a hangover, for example." I'm sure I've heard that somewhere. Seems kind of gross, but maybe it works.

The witch pulls out a small bag from under her cape. "I suppose I could do some experiments," she says. "Fine. One cup of hair of dog in exchange for a spell. Fair trade." She takes a small pair of scissors out of her bag.

I hold Rosa still while the witch cuts some hair off her tail and legs. Rosa is so fluffy, it's barely noticeable. The witch tucks the tufts of hair into her little bag.

"As for you…" She points at me. She has about three rings on every finger. "I have the potion you need right here." Digging in her bag again, she comes up with a small blue bottle. "One sip will be enough. Give some to the dog too. Unless you're leaving her behind."

"I'm not," I say.

"Shame," she says. "You won't be able to stay underwater forever. But it should be enough to get you safely through Merwood's swamp and up into the trees."

"Thank—" I start, but Salix kicks me. I forgot you're not supposed to thank Faeries. I guess the rule applies to witches too. "We're very gratef—" I don't finish that sentence either. The witch poofs back into smoke and disappears.

"That was strange," Finola says. "But I have good news and bad news."

"What now?" I ask.

"Well, the good news is that she, the witch, was a Faerie too. Some witches are. So she can't lie. Which means the potion she sold you will definitely work."

"That's a relief," Salix says.

"What's the bad news?" Indigo asks.

"The bad news is, the Wherewood has released me," Finola says. "I felt it as soon as the witch appeared. For some reason the Wherewood thinks the witch is what I was looking for. So I could leave now if I wanted to."

"Me too," says Indigo. "The Wherewood released me when I found my yo-yo."

"What?" I yell. "Indigo! That was ages ago. Why didn't you say something?"

Indigo shrugs. "I don't want to go home. This is fun."

I have to take a cleansing breath.

Salix puts his hand on my shoulder. "Maybe

they should stay with us until we find the entrance to Merwood. Then Indigo can slip them both back to Farwood."

"That might be safer," I admit. "Finola, do you mind?"

She looks uncomfortable. "I guess not," she says. "Indigo should go home. Oren will be furious. But..." She looks at Salix with sad eyes. "You're not going to stay in Merwood forever, are you?"

Indigo mimes barfing while Salix turns bright red through his green skin.

"Of course not," he says breathlessly. "I'll just say hello to my family and come back to you. I mean, to Farwood. Or to...wherever you are. Once I find Merwood, I should be able to slip in and out. Just like I did in the old days."

Finola smiles shyly, and everyone goes silent for so long that it gets very uncomfortable.

"Okay, let's keep going," I say when I can't stand it anymore. Rosa barks and tugs on her leash. Indigo skips ahead. I let Salix and Finola walk behind so I don't have to look at them holding hands and gawking at each other. Gross.

We tramp through more piles of lost socks and credit cards until the moon comes out. It gives us some light to see by. But it also makes weird shadows out of the trees. Finally the sky starts to brighten. The sun is rising. I can't believe we've been walking all night.

Through the trees we start to be able to see some mountains in the distance. Salix slows down and stares at them.

"I recognize this place!" he says. "That gorge there, see? We go through there!"

"Are you sure?"

"Yes!" Salix says. "Come on!"

He turns and runs toward the mountains. But before we've gone fifty feet, two dark shapes fall on us from the trees. I catch a glimpse of armor and know who it is. Olea's guards! I see the flash of a sword. Before I even know what is happening, I have the ghost sword out. I'm fighting.

Rosa growls and lunges at the guards. Finola's sword swipes through the branches. Salix's lantern cracks into an armored shoulder. Sparks and fire spray everywhere.

"Get behind me!" I shout, pulling Indigo back as a guard bears down on us. Indigo yelps and goes flying backward. My sword arcs through the air. But before it lands, Rosa leaps up and gets the guard by the throat. He screams. The other guard dives over and drags him away. Finola and Rosa chase the two guards through the trees. After a few seconds the guards sink down into the earth and disappear.

Salix runs toward me, breathless. "They slipped back to Nearwood," he says. "Oren told me there are still Nearwood Faeries who support Olea. She would have sent them here to look for us."

I put my sword away and turn back to check on Indigo.

He's curled up under a tree, holding his stomach.

His hands are covered with blood.

Chapter Seven

"Indigo!" I scream. I fall to my knees beside him.

"Blue…I'm hurt," he says.

Gently moving his hands, I see the wound. It's bad. A deep gash in his stomach. One of Olea's guards must have slashed him with a sword. Indigo grits his teeth and moans. He holds his hands back over his wound. A faint purple glow seeps out from under them.

Finola and Salix run up, Rosa behind them. Finola looks down at Indigo.

"No! Indigo, stop!" she yells.

"Stop what?" I ask.

Finola helps me lay him on his back. "He's trying a healing spell. But he's too young. It will use up all his magic."

The purple glow stops as Indigo lets his hands fall to his sides.

Rosa whines sadly, sniffing at Indigo's feet.

"He's already weak," Finola says. Her lips are pressed together. Her face is even paler than usual.

"Can one of you heal him?" I ask desperately. Indigo is crying now. I haven't seen him cry in years. His Grand Canyon T-shirt is soaked with blood.

"I'll try," Salix says. He holds his hands over Indigo. His healing light is green. It glows down on Indigo.

"Is it working?"

Salix ignores me. His face is scrunched up in concentration. I've never seen him look so serious. After a few seconds Indigo seems to settle. But Salix is sweating now. He loses his balance and stumbles backward.

"Salix!" Finola cries, catching him.

"I'm all right," he says, his voice raspy. "But that's all I can manage."

Indigo looks a bit better. But he's still bleeding. Finola lifts his shirt up and inspects the wound.

"It's partly healed," Finola says. "I'm worried that if I try to heal him, I'll use up all my magic. But we could slip right back to Farwood now instead. They have skilled healers there."

"You can do that?" I ask.

"Yes," Finola says. "Wherewood has released us both. And Indigo is a prince of Farwood. He can invite me."

My mind is spinning. It's so hard to keep Faerie laws straight. And who belongs to which kingdom.

But, as usual, Finola is being the most sensible. She's right.

I look back at Indigo. He's pale again. His eyes flutter.

"Indigo!" I shake him gently. "Finola, you better go right now. He's getting weaker."

Finola kneels next to him. She holds him around the shoulders.

"You have to invite me to Farwood, Indigo. Do it quickly," she says.

"Finola," Indigo murmurs weakly. "Finola MacLear, I invite you to the kingdom of Far...wood." His eyes close.

"Go now!" I say, tugging Salix back.

Finola looks up at Salix. "Be careful. And don't worry, Blue. I'll slip right into Oren's Great Hall. The healers will be there in seconds."

The ground starts to heave under them. Indigo moans with pain as they are sucked into the earth. Roots made of electrical cables and long scarves and knitting wool twist around them and pull them down. The jumble of mittens and socks and other lost things starts to close over them.

"Finola," Salix whispers beside me. But they're gone.

Salix and I stand there and stare at the ground for a long moment. I'm still shaking. My fear about Indigo's injury is turning to anger. Finally Salix speaks.

"What if I never see her again?" he says.

Something seems to crack open in my head. I spin around and glare at him.

"What if you never see *her* again?" I yell. "Are you serious? At least Finola's alive! Did you see my brother? He's half-dead because of you!"

Salix's froggy eyes widen. "I didn't know—"

I don't even let him finish. "Yes, you did! You knew it would be dangerous to come here. But you made me come with you anyway. And of course Indigo wanted to come along. He follows me everywhere."

Salix tries to interrupt. "The plan was—"

But I'm on a roll. I'm angry with everyone. At Oren for letting Indigo come along. At Indigo for going through the van into Wherewood without permission. At Olea for trying to kill us again.

But mostly I'm angry at Salix. He tricked me into making a deal with him. So I would owe him "something." And he could have asked for anything. Something safe, like a book or a batch of cookies. But instead he forced me to come along on this stupid quest. And now my brother has been stabbed.

And the worst thing is, I can't even leave Salix here. This stupid magical Faerie wood won't let me. Not until we find Merwood. I'm stuck with him.

"I don't care about the plan!" I say. "Plans are stupid even in the human world. In Faerieland they are worthless! Why do you even want to find Merwood now? Couldn't you wait?"

Salix hangs his head. "I'm sorry, Blue," he says. "I've messed everything up."

At least he admits it. But now I'm too mad to speak. I cross my arms.

"I promise I'll make it up to you," Salix says.

"Promise?" I say. "Like a *deal*? No thank you. Let's just find Merwood so I can go home."

I try to stomp away. But it's hard to stomp on ground made of lost mittens and socks. Salix follows me.

As we walk, I calm down. The strange Wherewood trees begin to clear. We get closer to the mountains. The sun is shining down on us. I dig in my backpack for one last yogurt tube and cheese stick and eat them, ignoring Salix. The mountains are farther away than I thought. By the time we reach them, the sun is behind their peaks. It's not dark yet. But we're walking in shadows.

Beside me, Salix murmurs something I don't quite hear.

"What?" I ask irritably.

"I said I need to find Merwood because if I don't, I can't grow up," Salix says.

I stop and stare at him. Rules and laws in Faerieland are all weird, but this one beats everything.

"I'm over one hundred years old," Salix explains. He looks down at his skinny, boyish body. "I've been like this for nearly ninety years. It's time for me to grow up. But I can't unless Merwood's high council grants it."

I try to make sense of that. "So...if you didn't want to grow up, you wouldn't have to?"

Salix nods. "Not for a long time anyway. But I *do* want to grow up. I think if I grow up I might stop being so...you know...messy."

I know he doesn't mean messy as in having an untidy room. He means messy as in nearly getting your friends killed. I wonder what I would do if I had the choice of whether to grow up or not. I don't enjoy being a teenager very much. But on the other hand, it might be nice to have enough time to get good at it. By the time I finish thinking about this, I'm not mad at Salix anymore. I feel sorry for him. I'm sure if I had to stay a kid for a hundred years I'd be messy too.

I'm about to apologize for yelling at him when he looks over my shoulder. His face lights up.

"What is it?" I ask, turning around.

"It's a Will-o'-the Wisp!" Salix says. "Come on!"

Chapter Eight

A Will-o'-the-Wisp! The witch had said they like swampy places. I am hoping they might show us the way to Merwood. Rosa and I run after Salix as he follows the tiny glowing light. It takes us down to a narrow creek. The creek cuts through the mountains. I see a crack of greenish light in the distance.

"That's it!" Salix says. "I know that! I recognize it!"

He starts to run. Rosa barks. We hurry to catch up to him. The gorge widens. The Will-o'-the-Wisp zips away into the bright light. Salix stops right where the rock cliffs open. The creek tumbles over the rocks in a waterfall.

A valley lies in front of us. The ground slopes down into the trees. It's a wild, green, steamy jungle. Colorful birds flutter through the branches.

"Is this Merwood?" I ask.

"No," Salix says. "But we're close. We just have to follow the creek. We're nearly there!"

Salix picks up Rosa and jumps off the cliff with her. He lands gracefully in the thick undergrowth below us. I have to climb down the rocks under the waterfall.

Once I'm at the bottom, we start to follow the burbling creek into the jungle. The trees close in around us.

"We're not in Wherewood anymore?" I ask.

"No," Salix says. He's smiling brightly, excited. "I mean, kind of. This is part of the Crosswood. It's a place where you can cross into Merwood. But this crossing was lost when Merwood was cursed."

"A hundred years ago?" I ask.

"Exactly," Salix says. "During the war, some of us escaped into the Crosswood. To be safe. But then—"

"A whole chunk of the Crosswood just disappeared?" I ask. "You lost your way back home?"

Salix looks sad again. It's messed up that things like war and refugees happen in the Faerie world too. You'd think being able to do magic, they'd be nicer to each other. I guess not.

Salix tugs back a thick bundle of fronds.

"This is it!" he cries, pushing through the leaves. Before Rosa and I even get through, I hear a splash.

We emerge at the edge of a perfectly round pond. Trees form a canopy over it, like a roof. Salix is paddling around. His face is a picture of happiness.

"So what do we do?" I ask him. "We just dive down?"

"Yes!" he says. "Don't forget to drink your potion. Then dive in and follow me!"

The potion is in my backpack. I dig it out and pour a sip into my palm. Rosa laps it up easily. Then I drink the rest.

All I feel is a kind of *green* sensation. And a very strong urge to get into the water. Rosa tugs on her leash. We both dive in.

I can see clearly under the water. Salix is at the center of the pond. He's about ten feet under the surface. Rosa dives deeper and swims toward him, pulling me along.

There's a glowing green light coming from the bottom of the pond. Salix flips over and swims down into the water. I think about going up to take a breath. But then I do take a breath. Of water! I'm breathing underwater!

We swim after Salix, into the green light.

→ ★ ←

It's kind of like traveling through the ground into the Crosswood. Only this time it's vines and pondweeds that tangle around us. In seconds we pop out on the other side.

Through the weeds I see Salix literally dancing with joy underwater. He swirls and swoops like a dolphin. His mouth is open in a wide, happy grin.

This must be Merwood!

Rosa barks out a cloud of bubbles and paddles after him.

Suddenly a dark green weed slithers up from the bottom of the pond. It winds around Rosa's neck. I push through the water, trying to grab for her. But the weed pulls her down! Her leash slips from my hand!

"Salix!" I yell underwater.

He spins. His eyes go wide.

One of the weeds curls around my ankle. I fight against it. I grab Rosa by her furry scruff, but the weeds still have us. I try to reach for the ghost sword, but my wrist is tangled.

The weeds yank us down. I catch a glimpse of Salix getting caught too.

The weeds suck us into complete darkness. I cling desperately to Rosa's fur. It's the only thing that seems real. Finally we are flung violently out of the water. We land in a tangle of vines. The vines slither and wrap around us.

"Salix!" I yell. "Salix!"

Rosa barks and clambers into my lap as the vines completely capture us.

"Where are we?" I say. "Salix? Are you here?"

We seem to be in a dark forest made of oily,

tangled vines. The ground feels like sludge. And it smells rotten. Like a compost heap.

Rosa whines. I try to wrap my arms around her. "Are you okay, girl? Are you hurt?"

"Blue?" a voice says. I know that voice. I can't believe it.

"Violet?"

A little golden head pokes out of the tangle of vines wrapped around the next tree. "Blue!" Violet says. "How did you get here?"

"How did *you* get here?" I ask. "You're supposed to be in Nearwood." Violet has a whole squadron of guards in Nearwood. They're to keep enemies away from her but also to keep her from running off. Which I just know is what she did.

"Someone grabbed me in the Crosswood," she says. "I was sneaking back to Mom's place to get my calculator."

"Your calculator? Violet! You can't sneak around Faerieland on your own. You can't sneak anywhere on your own. Why didn't you send a messenger or something?"

Violet sulks. "I'm not allowed to have a calculator. Oren is teaching me number spells. But he wants me to add things in my head."

I sigh. Even as the queen of Nearwood, Violet is a brat. It's amazing.

Twisting in the vines, I manage to get my hand on the hilt of my sword. I swish it out and cut through the vines. Rosa and I flop onto the ground.

"Whose dog is that?" Violet asks as I cut through her vines.

"Long story," I say. "Is Salix here?"

"I haven't seen him," Violet says. "I've been here for hours."

"It was Olea," I say angrily. "I know it. Somehow she got to us. She tried in the Wherewood. But this time she succeeded."

Violet looks grim. The dark forest seems to press in around us.

"If Olea did this, then she might have Salix with her," Violet says. "And the only place she could be is in Witherwood."

Chapter Nine

Witherwood. Even the name gives me the creeps. Witherwood is like a prison for bad Faeries. I don't know much else about it. Olea was sent there "hereafter and ever after." Forever, in other words. It was punishment for killing Oren's father. He was Olea's husband for a time. Violet and Indigo are their children.

Families in Faerieland are *complicated*.

"We have to rescue Salix!" I say desperately. I know a few hours ago I was mad at him. But I'm over that now. "Can we get into Witherwood? Where are we anyway?"

Violet looks very serious. "This is Fenwood," she says.

"Fenwood? That's one of the woods that was cursed after the war, right?"

She nods solemnly. "Merwood's curse has expired. But Fenwood was cursed for a thousand years. It still has nine hundred years to go."

I look around at the drooping, oily vines and spindly trees. It's not cold, but I get a chill. Rosa whines and presses into my leg.

"What does it mean to be cursed?" I ask.

"I'm not sure," Violet answers. "But I've heard that some of the Faeries who are still loyal to Olea have come here."

This is terrible news. Violet took Olea's crown. She took the throne of Nearwood and banished

Olea to Witherwood. If there are Faeries here still loyal to Olea, they will want Violet dead.

"We need to get you out of here," I say.

"Not before we rescue Salix," Violet says. "As a queen of the Faerie Woods, I am responsible for him."

I don't even try to argue with her. Where Indigo is impulsive, Violet is stubborn. And anyway, I want to rescue Salix too.

"How will we get into Witherwood?" I ask. "Is it hard?"

"Not hard," Violet says. "But it might be dangerous."

"What isn't in Faerieland?" I say.

Violet smirks. "True enough," she says. "We need to look for a Faerie circle. I don't think one will be hard to find here." She looks around uneasily and shivers. I slip my hoodie off and give it to her. She puts it on without a word. It's much too big on her. But at least she'll be warm.

"What are we looking for?" I ask as we start picking our way through the vines. "What does a Faerie circle look like?"

"It's a circle of mushrooms or toadstools," Violet says. "They like damp, dark places. Look under fallen logs or in shadows."

Violet is right. Not ten minutes have passed when we find a perfect circle of vile-looking mushrooms in a clearing.

"Now what?" I ask.

"Now we jump in," Violet says. "We should hold hands."

I take Violet's hand in one of mine. With my other hand I hold on to Rosa's shaggy scruff. We jump into the circle.

Nothing happens.

"I was afraid of that," Violet says. "I think we might need to eat the mushrooms."

"Eat them?" I know about eating wild mushrooms. How it's usually a very bad idea. With our living in the forest, it is something Mom warned me against. "What if they're poisonous?"

"They won't be poisonous," Violet says. "The Faerie Woods aren't like that. But they will be magical. Anyway, I have an antidote spell. Oren taught it to Indigo and me. In case you ever accidentally ate Faerie food."

"That was thoughtful of him," I say. "Okay then. Let's do it."

Violet picks three mushrooms. She swallows hers quickly. I eat mine and give the last one to Rosa. She chomps it down.

Almost immediately my vision goes funny. Rosa growls and shakes her head like she has something in her ear.

"Ready now," Violet says. "Take my hand."

I grab her hand and Rosa's scruff.

And we jump.

Yep. That worked. The oily, damp forest disappears. We're plunged into darkness. Nothingness. It lasts a long, long time. I can't move or speak. Or see. Or hear. Thank goodness I can still feel Violet's hand in mine. And Rosa's scruff. If not for that, I think I'd go mad.

At last I feel something else. It's a terrible pain in my stomach. Rosa howls as I bend over and throw up. I blink, and the world comes into focus. I'm kneeling on the ground. Poor Rosa is retching and vomiting next to me.

Violet helps me stand.

"I'm sorry, Blue!" she cries. "I had no idea it would take so long. You've been in a kind of trance. Rosa too."

"What?" I ask.

Violet has tears on her face. "I tried the antidote spell as soon as we got through," she says. "But maybe it wasn't strong enough or…I don't know. You've just been standing there like a zombie for ages. Then you fell down and started barfing!"

I take a step. My bones and muscles are stiff. "For how long?" I ask.

"Hours!" Violet says tearfully. "I thought you were going to die!"

Then she starts to cry again. I loop Rosa's leash around my wrist and gather both of them into a group hug.

When we're all feeling better, I look around. Now I can see that we're in the strangest forest I've been in yet. Instead of trees there are only shadows. Like ghost trees. And the ground is completely smooth and gray. There's no undergrowth, no moss. Nothing. It's like a polished stone floor. The air smells…electric. Like just before a thunderstorm. And there's no sun that I can see. The light is dim and hazy. It comes from glowing patches on the trees.

We're in Witherwood. There is no doubt in my mind.

"We need to find Salix," I say. "Now."

We don't have to look for long. But it's long enough for me to know I never want to come to Witherwood again. Strange creatures peer at us as we walk. Bony hands reach out from behind the shadow trees. Rosa growls at them and they retreat. Stepping over a deep trench—maybe it's a grave— we're confronted by three dim figures. They're very tall and almost transparent.

"Let me pass," Violet says bravely. "I'm Queen of Nearwood."

The figures drift away like living cobwebs.

Finally we come upon Olea's court. Or at least the court she's trying to have. It's in a clearing surrounded by foul-smelling torches. They burn with blue flames and give off thick red smoke. Olea sits in the center on a throne made of jagged rocks.

Three guards stand behind her. Instead of swords they have rough stone axes that look handmade.

In front of Olea, a large bubble of water hovers in midair.

Salix is floating inside the bubble! As I step into the clearing, he drifts around and sees me. He presses his hands on the sides of the bubble. It's like some kind of fish tank. And he's trapped!

"Let him go," I say.

Olea looks at me, bored.

"Took you long enough," she says. "What will you give me if I free your little froggy friend?"

I rest my hand on the hilt of my ghost sword. "I'm not playing that game with you," I say.

"Shame," she says. "Little froggy will need to breathe air soon."

I draw my sword. Olea's guards step forward, axes raised.

"Blue, no!" Violet says. She yanks me back.

Salix twitches inside the bubble. His cheeks puff out. He needs air.

"It's me you want," Violet says to Olea. "If you let Salix go, I'll stay here in Witherwood."

"What?" I yell. "Viol—"

But Olea says, "Deal."

The shadowy trees shimmer. I know what that means. The Faerie Woods have accepted the pact.

The bubble pops, spraying water everywhere. Salix lands in a wet pile, gasping for air. He's alive, at least.

But now Violet is stuck here in Witherwood.

Chapter Ten

Once the deal is done, Olea and her guards lose interest in us. Violet and I help Salix up and drag him away. Rosa follows us, barking. No one tries to stop us. We retreat through the shadowy trees. I want to get as far away from Olea as possible. Then we need to talk about what to do.

"You and Salix could leave," Violet says. "There's no magic keeping you here. Once Salix is strong enough, you should be able to slip back to—"

"No," I say quickly. "I'm not leaving you here. We are not even discussing that."

Down a hill, by a creek that runs with sickly gray water, we find a small cave. Violet flicks a spark of magic inside, lighting it up. The cave is empty. It looks relatively dry and safe.

Exhausted and weak, Salix curls up and goes to sleep. Violet waves sparkles from the tips of her fingers over the cave entrance—some kind of protective magic.

"You should sleep too," she says when she's done. "I'll keep watch."

I don't answer. I just let her crawl out of the cave and sit at the entrance. She knows how angry I am at her for making a deal with Olea. She knows I don't want to talk.

I try to sleep. When that fails, I try to calculate how many hours I've been awake. But it's impossible. Days and nights have lost all meaning.

I have to get Violet out of here. The problem is, this is the Faerie world. In my world I might be able to call the police or child protective services. If we were in Farwood or the Crosswood, we might be able to get help from Oren.

But this is Witherwood. I don't think any rules apply here. I just don't know enough. Even though I'm still furious with her, I need to talk to Violet.

She looks back at me as I crawl out of the cave.

"I left Rosa watching Salix," I say.

She nods, looking at the gloomy forest of shadows.

"I should have known this would happen," Violet says.

"What?" I don't know what she's talking about.

"Olea has made herself Queen of Witherwood," Violet says tightly. "I should have predicted that. I didn't think it was possible."

"What does that mean?" I ask.

Violet sighs. "Faeries get their magic from the woods. If a wood accepts someone as king or queen, that Faerie becomes powerful."

"Olea is Queen of Witherwood?" I ask. This is more terrible news.

"She must be," Violet says. "Otherwise how could she capture us? Or put Salix into that bubble? She should barely be able to do magic at all."

I think about this. "But if becoming king or queen of a wood makes someone powerful, you must be powerful, Violet. You're Queen of Nearwood."

"I am powerful," she admits. "But I don't know how to use it yet. Half the time, things just catch fire. Or explode. Or disappear."

"If only I could command Olea again," I say.

"You can't," Violet reminds me. "You used up your three wishes with her. And that magic only works once."

"What if I commanded Salix or you to get us out of here?" I ask.

"Salix is still too weak, even for that kind of magic," Violet says. "And heaven knows what my magic would do. Anyway I'm not sure the wood would allow it. Or it might decide that killing us is a way of getting us out of here."

I take a slow breath. Magic is dangerous. I have to remember that.

"If only there was another human here," I say. "One who hasn't commanded Olea yet."

Violet makes a little huffing noise. She hugs her knees, wrapping herself in my hoodie.

Then I get an idea. A terrifying one.

An hour later a kind of dawn arrives. The dim gray light in Witherwood brightens a bit. Salix stirs in the cave. Rosa gives a hopeful yip. I search in the bottom of my backpack. All I find are a few cupcake crumbs and a cereal bar I missed. Rosa eats the crumbs and half of the cereal bar. I eat the other half.

Violet manages to magically conjure some very weird-looking apples. She and Salix eat them, making faces.

"Sour," Salix says.

Violet and I formulated a plan last night. It's *bonkers*. But it might work. And we have no other choice. I consider explaining it to Salix. But then I decide it might be better if he doesn't know. He'd probably try to talk me out of it. It's dangerous. That's why we're leaving it to the last minute.

Before we go, we arm ourselves. Salix gathers rocks from the creek, filling his pockets. He fashions a sling with strips cut from my hoodie. Violet uses magic to turn a thin weed into a sharp piece of metal. She only sets three small fires before she gets it right. I have my ghost sword. I tighten the belt with the scabbard and rest my hand on the hilt as we walk.

We have to take our time. Salix is still recovering from his ordeal in the water bubble. He was already weak because of all the magic he used trying to heal

Indigo. After a few minutes we stop so he can catch his breath.

"You can stay behind," I say. "Rosa could stay with you."

He glares at me. "After what Olea did to me?" he says sharply. "I wouldn't miss this for all the lily pads in Merwood. Besides, she has three guards. Plus her is four. We have you, me, Rosa and Violet. Four against four."

A weakened Faerie, a junior Faerie, a human and a dog. Against three full-grown guards and the queen of Witherwood.

If not for the bonkers plan, I would think we didn't have a hope.

I wish there were a way I could get a message to Mom. There's a chance, a good chance, that I'm going to die trying what we've planned. Then Salix and Violet will be stuck here and Mom won't ever know what happened to us. Maybe Finola got Indigo to Oren's court. Hopefully, Oren's healers fixed him. He could tell Mom what he knows. She'd figure out the rest.

I think since the moment she made the first deal with Olea—the one that saved my life when I was four—she must have thought something would happen one day. I realize now my poor mother has been living with this all these years. She has known that Faerie magic was a constant risk.

I wish I could just apologize to her. This is all my fault. I lost the twins in the woods that day. That's when Oren grabbed them. That's when this all started.

"It'll be okay," Violet says. She must be reading my mood. It probably shows on my face.

None of the creatures of Witherwood try to stop us as we approach Olea's court. What passes for a sun here—a dull gray orb in the sky—has risen. It casts everything in cold, harsh light. The shadow trees are more distinct now. Slowing to examine one, I see it's covered in tiny spines, like a cactus. I carefully steer clear as we continue.

Finally the clearing becomes visible through the haze. Olea is still sitting on her jagged throne. Her guards linger around her. The torches spew rancid smoke.

Olea looks up as we enter the clearing.

"The band of travelers returns," she says snidely. "Come to beg for breakfast?"

I draw my sword. Salix loads his slingshot. Rosa crouches back and growls. Violet raises her blade. The guards step toward us.

"Now?" I ask.

"Now," Violet says.

And I shout, "VIOLET NASH PANASH BUCKTHORN BRIAR BRAMBLE, I COMMAND YOU: GIVE UP YOUR MAGIC!"

Chapter Eleven

"NO!" Olea shouts.

Suddenly everyone, me included, is frozen in place. Violet's head is tilted back. Her arms are flung up like she's falling. Sparks of magic fly out of her open mouth. And from her fingertips. And from her ears. Her face is frozen in a terrified scream.

If this stupid idea kills Violet, I'll never forgive myself. I will never leave Witherwood, even if I could.

I'll crawl into a corner and die. I try to reach for her, but I can't move. The magic pours out of her, now in fiery streams of light that dash around the clearing. They slam into Olea and her guards, bouncing off in all directions.

I know what is happening. The escaping magic—wild magic—is looking for something non-magical to fill. It floods the clearing, whooshing out between the trees before twisting back. It bounces off Salix, making him yelp.

I can't help it. I close my eyes. I might not need to forgive myself. Maybe I'll just die right now.

When the magic hits me, it's like diving into boiling water. I try to scream. But all that happens is my mouth fills with fire. Then I feel like I'm being burned from the inside out. Everything goes white for a second. I can't see anything or hear anything. Maybe I am dead.

Suddenly my senses all rush back. I open my eyes and look around. The clearing looks different.

The colors are brighter. The details on the trees, the throne and the sky are clearer. Is this how Faeries see? I can hear Rosa panting next to me. And Salix breathing. And Violet. We're all still alive.

But so is Olea.

"Kill the girl!" she screams to her guards. Her hands fly up, and a shock wave of magic blows past us. The trees around the clearing explode! Fragments of dark, spindly bark fly everywhere and...oh...oh no...

Spiders! Olea has turned the trees into thousands of huge spiders!

They swarm over Violet. The plan was to turn Violet into a human. I commanded her to give up her magic by using her full name. Now that she's a human, she can command Olea.

But no one can give commands with spiders scrawling over their face! Violet screams and falls to the ground. Rosa leaps on her, snapping at the spiders.

Olea's guards rush forward, their axes raised. My ghost sword flies down on one of them, slicing his ax in half. Salix fires stones from his slingshot. They clang against the guard's helmets, stunning them.

"The girl!" Olea repeats. "Get the girl!"

As Violet crawls out of the mass of spiders, I feel her magic surging up in me. I don't know the first thing about casting spells, but I shoot my hand out. Spreading my fingers, I concentrate on one thought— *protect Violet.*

Sparks fly out from my fingertips. They streak across the clearing and swirl around Violet. Spiders pop and disappear like tiny fireworks as the sparks touch them. The swirl of sparks turns into a kind of dome. It settles over Violet like a protective shield. Finally she struggles to her feet, brushing away dead spiders.

My hand starts to shake. I'm not sure how much longer I can keep up this magic, whatever it is.

"Now, Violet!" I yell. "NOW!"

Olea starts to run. But Violet roars after her.

"OLEA NASH PANASH BUCKTHORN BRIAR BRAMBLE, I COMMAND YOU: GIVE UP YOUR MAGIC!"

Everything freezes again. My protective spell dissolves. The dome of magic around Violet collapses.

Olea's head and arms fly back. "NOOOOOOO!" she screams.

But it's no use. Her magic pours out of her. I watch in horror as the flaming streams dash around the clearing. They blast into me, Salix and the guards. After an instant of searing heat they bounce off. The streams gather above the clearing in a tangle. With a roar they shoot down to where Violet stands. A flash of power slams into her so hard she flies backward. Rosa yelps and goes sailing back with her.

Olea wails with rage. Drawing a knife, she storms across the clearing.

I'm still partially frozen. I struggle against the

magic, trying to reach Violet before Olea does. Rosa pounces on Olea, growling. Olea slashes at her.

"No!" Violet yells. She shoves her hands forward, and a huge bolt of light zooms out. Olea's own magic! It hits Olea with an earsplitting boom. The flash blinds me. It seems to fill the clearing like a massive explosion.

When it clears, Olea is gone. Violet is standing there, gasping for breath, her arms still outstretched. Salix is struggling to his feet across the clearing. Olea's guards are running for their lives.

And Rosa is lying on the hard ground, bloodied. She's not moving.

$$\rightarrow \bigstar \leftarrow$$

"No!" I cry. "Rosa!"

The magic finally releases me. I run, falling on my knees beside her. The fur over Rosa's neck and shoulder is soaked with blood.

"No, no, no," I whisper. I turn to Violet. "Help her!"

Violet holds out her hands. A few sparks trickle from her fingers. But nothing happens.

"It was the explosion," she says. "I'm sorry. I don't know what I did. I used up too much of Olea's magic. I can't do a healing spell."

"Salix?"

He staggers across the clearing. "I'm still weak. If I try, I might use up all my magic too," he says. "And we'll be stuck here."

I look around, desperate. In the distance, through the trees, I can see Olea's guards trailing back, axes raised. I slide my hands under Rosa's still body. My vision goes blurry with tears.

"Get us out of here," I say, trying not to sob.

"Nearwood Castle," Violet says. "I can invite you there."

"I don't trust Nearwood right now," Salix says. "No offense."

The guards stomp back into the clearing.

"Now, Salix!" I yell. "Anywhere!"

He grabs us. The hard ground of Witherwood cracks and shatters. It churns into a pit of gravel. Then we sink. Sharp chunks of broken stone and gravel scratch and dig into my skin. My eyes fill with dust. At last the ground spits us out on the other side.

I roll over. Staggering to my feet with Rosa in my arms, I look around.

"Salix!" Violet cries. "This is the Wherewood again!"

She's right. Though it's now dark, I can see the trees are hung with wallets and keys. My feet are tangled in phone-charger cables.

"I was trying for the Crosswood!" Salix says.

"We just need to find the way out," I say. "The van. That's what we're all looking for, right? If we find it, the Wherewood will release us."

"What about Rosa?" Violet says.

I hold Rosa tight. I can feel her little heart beating really fast. She's still alive, but barely.

Suddenly a figure appears in the distance. It runs toward us, waving a flaming torch. We press back when the figure bursts through the trees.

It's Harriet Tubman again! Her face is stern in the torchlight.

"Rebel or Unionist?" she asks me in a low voice.

I say the first thing I think of. "I'm Canadian."

"Canada?" she says, pointing with her torch. "This way!"

We follow her because what else can we do? A minute later I spot something in the gloom. Something yellow. Is that...?

"It's the van!" Salix says. "It's the way out!"

"Freedom," Harriet Tubman says. "Follow the North Star!" She disappears in a cloud of homework sheets just before we reach the van.

Salix throws the door open. He steps back to let me clamber through with Rosa. Violet follows. Salix goes last. The van door slams behind him.

The door on the other side opens. The fresh, happy smell of the Crosswood greets me. I climb out carefully. Salix and Violet join me as I lay Rosa on the ground. Normal leafy, mossy ground at last!

Violet grabs my arm as I let my hands hover over Rosa's wounds.

"Blue," she says. "A healing spell will use all the wild magic you've got. You'll never get any back."

"I don't care," I say. "I have to help her. She saved your life. She saved all of us."

Salix takes my shoulder. Violet takes the other one. They encourage me as they hold me up.

"Think about Rosa's life," Salix instructs me. "Think about how much you love her. Turn that into magic."

My fingers start to tingle, then burn. Sparks of blue light drift down and settle on Rosa's fur. She stirs.

"It's working!" Violet says.

The blue light intensifies into a bright glow. It covers Rosa's whole body. Soon the light is pulsing in time with her heartbeat. It becomes stronger. Rosa's eyes open. She whines and moves her head.

I can feel the last dregs of wild magic leave me. I hope it's enough. It has to be enough! There's a flash, and I reel back. The soft ground cushions me as I fall.

"Blue!" Salix says.

My vision goes dim for a second. I hear a hearty bark. Fluffy paws land on my chest. A warm tongue licks my face.

I open my eyes to see Rosa grinning and drooling over me. She yips and licks me again.

"Ugh, Rosa," I say. "Your breath *smells*."

Chapter Twelve

Oren is *furious.* He and Finola find us in the Crosswood not long after we get back there. Violet is grounded. Indigo is grounded. Salix only avoids being thrown in the dungeon by inviting Finola to Merwood. She slips them both away when Oren isn't watching. I expect they'll avoid Oren and Farwood for quite some time.

After we spend another night at his castle, Oren escorts Rosa and me back to the Crosswood.

"Olea is probably not dead," he says as we near the right place—the crossing to the forest behind Mom's house. "Likely the powerful spell that Violet cast was an expulsion spell. She cast Olea out of the Faerie Woods altogether."

"What does that mean?" I ask. "Where is she?"

"In the human realm somewhere," Oren says. "Overwood, we call it. Earth. But she could be anywhere on Earth. I understand it's not very easy for you humans to travel around."

"No," I say. I don't like the idea of Olea being in the human world. Even without her magic, I don't trust her. "But she's definitely not magical anymore, right?"

"Definitely," Oren says. "But she's clever and devious. You will need to be on guard."

Unbelievably, my first thought is wishing again that I was magic. But I push that thought away. I've nearly died from magic a hundred times in the last few days. I've learned my lesson.

Oren says goodbye and slips me and Rosa through to Mom's forest. When I get back to our cottage, Mom greets me with hugs and muffins. She digs out an old pan and fills it with water for Rosa. Rosa laps it happily and then eats a peanut butter sandwich.

"We'll have to get dog food," Mom says. "You're sure she's a normal dog, right? She's not a Faerie dog?"

"They don't have dogs in Faerieland," I say. "But we should try to find her owner."

Later, Mom drives us into the city, to the address on the envelope Rosa had in her mouth. Somehow it has survived in my pocket. It's damp and scrunched, but still readable.

The address takes us to a little house on a corner by a gas station. Mom waits in the car while I knock on the door. A gray-haired man answers.

"Is there a Rosa Guzman here?" I ask.

"Guzman?" the man says. "The Guzmans owned this house forty years ago. I bought it from them."

"Forty years?" I ask. "Do you know where they are?"

"They'd be long dead," the man says. "They were elderly when I moved in."

I look down at Rosa. She doesn't seem to recognize the man.

"I found this dog," I say. I show the man the scrunched-up letter. "She had this letter with her."

The man takes the letter and examines it. "Huh," he says. "This is an old phone bill. But the company changed its name back in the eighties."

Rosa huffs and rests her head against my knee, gazing up at me.

"Do you recognize this dog?" I ask. "Do you know whose dog she is?"

The old man smiles. "By the look on her face, I'd say she's *your* dog, son," he says.

Rosa barks, as though she agrees.

Mom just rolls her eyes when I tell her what the man said. Then we stop at the pet store on the way back out to the cottage. Rosa gets food, and a proper collar and leash, and a raincoat, and a bowl and a bed. We hit the walk-in vet clinic in our town. The vet says he thinks Rosa is about two years old, but she doesn't have a microchip. He gives her one, and some shots. And he books her in to get "fixed" in two weeks.

Mom says I have to do chores for our neighbor Mrs. Chen to help pay for all this. I don't mind though. Rosa is worth it.

⇒ ★ ⇐

Violet and Indigo come home for the weekend. They are both unusually subdued. I think being locked in their rooms in Oren's castle for half the week has worked a kind of magic on them. Indigo even rinses out the bathtub after using it. Violet helps Mom fold laundry. It's a miracle.

Mom leaves me with them to go work a shift at her job in town. Violet colors in an incredibly complicated coloring book. Indigo tries to gross her out by reading passages from a book about mold. It doesn't work.

"I've been to Witherwood, Indigo," she says. "Nothing could be grosser than that."

Indigo gives up. He starts on his own coloring book. Mom says if they color every page, she'll let us borrow a DVD player from the library.

An hour later we're all hungry. There's nothing in the house but vegetables, rice and oats.

"I have an idea, Blue," Violet says. "I'm magic again because Olea's wild magic fixed me. And you still have two commands left. Why don't you command me to conjure a cheese pizza?"

I really shouldn't. But of course I do. For one thing, I want to see if I'm back to being fully human again. I must be, because it works. In seconds we are stuffing ourselves with pizza. We wash it down with homemade carrot juice. That's healthy, right?

I'm glad that Olea's wild magic turned Violet back into a Faerie. I wasn't sure it would. But Oren told me it worked just like a blood transfusion would. It healed her. And her Faerie body can now keep making magic. Just like it did before.

Violet makes much more sense as a Faerie than she would as a human.

I use the remaining command to make Violet wash the dishes. She probably would have anyway. But I want to get the last wish out of the way.

I don't need to command Indigo to dry the dishes. A threat to tell Oren he misbehaved is enough.

As they work, I lie back on the sofa and relax. Rosa jumps on top of me. I try to shove her off.

"Rosa, get down," I say. She doesn't budge. My ribs creak from her weight. I think she's gained ten pounds since we got home.

"Rosa, oof. You're crushing me. Get off." She just licks my face. I try to squirm away, but that makes her more determined. "Rosa...no...Rosa...stop..." I don't know why I say what I do next. Maybe just habit.

"Mrs. Rosa Guzman, I command you: Get off me and go outside!"

Rosa freezes. Her body floats up off me and lands gracefully on the floor.

"What the...?" Indigo says, turning from the sink.

Rosa woofs and trots obediently over to the door. The *closed* door. It unlocks and swings open.

Rosa bounds outside. Indigo, Violet and I follow her, watching from the porch as she frolics in the yard. It's getting dark, and we can clearly see Rosa playing with what looks like fireflies. They're not fireflies, of course. I know she's playing with Will-o'-the-Wisps. Just like Indigo and Violet used to.

"That's...odd," Violet says.

"It's awesome," Indigo says.

I don't say anything.

Either some of Violet's magic or some of Olea's magic must have gotten into Rosa. Oren told me that when wild magic gets into a human, it is quickly used up. And humans can't make any more. But does that apply to dogs?

Because if it doesn't, I just used up one of her three commands. I now have a magical dog.

That sounds awesome, as Indigo says, but, knowing me, it will end in disaster.

What else is new?

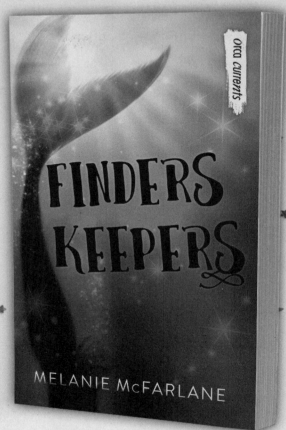

I stood up quickly. I looked down at my feet to make sure there was nothing near them. That's when I spotted something sparkly under the water. I had to investigate. Finding things is kind of my thing. I started digging carefully like I'd learned from my handbook, *Treasure Hunting 101*. Rule number one: Always protect the scene.

My fingers found something solid. It felt like a bottle. I pulled it out of the sand and held it over my head like a trophy. I had found the first treasure of the day!

"Hey!" Sam called out. "What's that?" He ran into the water and stood next to me.

"Aw," said my little brother, joining us. "It's just a bottle."

"Hang on," I said. Something clinked inside the bottle.

I flipped the bottle over. With a *THUNK*, a blob of wet sand fell out. Stuck inside the bottle was a beautiful pink shell that glimmered. I tried to shake it out.

"Whoa, that's cool," Sam said. "I've never seen a shell like that before."

"Maybe it's from the ocean!" my brother said.

"That's impossible, Bug," I said. My brother is eight years old. His real name is Ben. Mom thinks I call him Bug because he likes creepy crawlers. But really it's because he's so annoying, a real pain in my butt. I always have to babysit him.

"Is not," Bug said. He crossed his arms.

I grunted. The closest ocean is more than a thousand miles away. But Bug had a point. This shell did *not* look like any of the brown clamshells I'd found at the bottom of the lake.

I shrugged. "Lost treasure?"

We made our way back to the beach. Sam and Bug followed me up to the rocky ledge where we'd left our bags and bikes. Close to Mrs. Wilson's cabin, it was the perfect place to stash our stuff, away from the crowds of people on the beach.

Bug pushed between us. "How did that big shell get in that tiny opening anyway?" he asked.

"Beat it, Bug." I peered into the bottle. I'd seen a ship in a bottle before, down at the Treasure Trove, the local general store. But someone had built that boat inside the bottle, piece by piece. Bug was right. How did a shell get inside this one?

"But I want to see," said Bug.

He grabbed at the bottle. I lost my grip, and the bottle fell out of my hands. It smashed against the rocky shore. Glass shot everywhere, like sparks at a campfire. The shell slid between two rocks, just out of reach.

"Bug!" I yelled. "Look what you did."

Bug stepped back, crossing his arms again and pinching his lips together. "I'm going to tell Mom you're not being nice."